Where Is Christmas, Jesse Bear?

Where Is Christmas, Jesse Bear?

by **Nancy White Carlstrom**

illustrated by **Bruce Degen**

SCHOLASTIC INC.

New York Toronto London Auckland Sydney
Mexico City New Delhi Hong Kong

ISBN 0-439-30549-7

Text copyright © 2000 by Nancy White Carlstrom.
Illustrations copyright © 2000 by Bruce Degen.
All rights reserved. Published by Scholastic Inc.,
555 Broadway, New York, NY 10012, by arrangement
with Simon & Schuster Books for Young Readers,
Simon & Schuster Children's Publishing Division.
SCHOLASTIC and associated logos are trademarks
and/or registered trademarks of Scholastic Inc.

12 11 10 9 8 7 6 5 4 3 2 1   1 2 3 4 5 6/0

Printed in the U.S.A.   24

First Scholastic printing, November 2001

Book design by Anahid Hamparian

The text for this book is set in 18-point Goudy.
The illustrations are rendered in pen-and-ink and watercolor.

For Caleb and Tracy Richardson
in celebration of Christmas and skiing
—JESSE BEAR AND N. W. C.

To the Bostard family,
who really *showed me where Christmas is*
—B. D.

Where is Christmas, Jesse Bear?
I see Christmas over there.
Marching to the door
Knock knock boom.
Come on in, Christmas,
We'll make room.

Decorations from the attic
Spilling down the stairs,
Strings of lights and snowflakes,
Garland-covered chairs.

Where is Christmas, Jesse Bear?
I touch Christmas over there.
Baubles on the branches,
Needles on the tree,
Scratchy, smooth, and prickly,
Tickling you and me.

Sticking on the stamps,
Marking off the days,
Wrapping all the gifts
For family far away.

Where is Christmas, Jesse Bear?
I smell Christmas over there.
Baking in the kitchen,
Fudge and gingerbears,
Hot, spicy apple cider
Steaming up the air.

Lemon sugar cookies,
Stars and Christmas trees,
Cinnamon and sprinkles
Decorating me!

Where is Christmas, Jesse Bear?
I hear Christmas over there.
Clanging at the shops,
Singing on the street,
Humming merry music,
Drumming with my feet.

Winding up the music box,
Playing of the chimes,
Ringing of the sleigh bells—
Jingle-jangle time.

Where is Christmas, Jesse Bear?
I know Christmas moves out there.
Shopping with the crowds,
Skating in the park,
Moving house to house
Caroling in the dark.

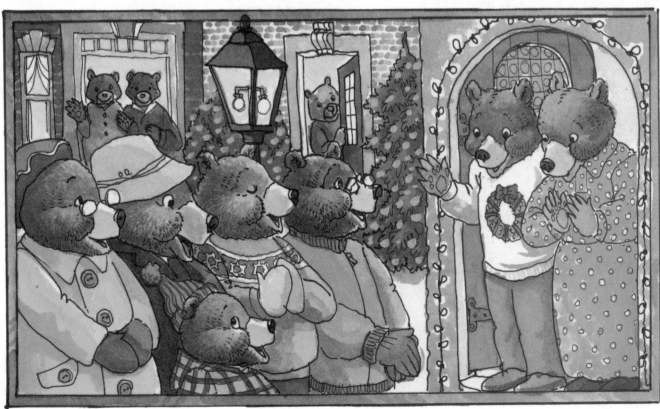

Prancing with the reindeer,
Grazing with the sheep,
Flying with the angel wings,
Wiggle-jiggle leap!

Where is Christmas, Jesse Bear?
I feel Christmas everywhere.
Warming up my heart,
Lighting up your face,
Joy to the world,
Peace in this place.

Shining in the candles,
Snuggling in the chair,
Snowing on the outside—
It's here, Jesse Bear!

Christmas is here!